ÚATH

Siân Posy

ÚATH

Úath

ISBN: 978-1-8383283-3-7

For the Square

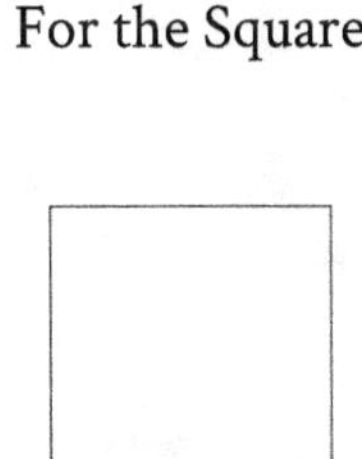

I would live for you

ÚATH

i

A Visiting

ii

Water From The Well

iii

Leviathan

iv

Solve Coagula

v

6C

vi

Un-Me

A VISITING

Being not afraid is a naïveté. Having your home entered by a stranger is an affront. The dead of the night is no friendly invitation for an unknown creature at your door. This door in particular was draped canvas, which blew gently in the wind over the mountain. The air was dry from the looming desert breath and still the night brought a chill through the shelter; rattling rocks blew into the sheets where the sleeper shivered in the cold. Being not afraid was something they were not accustomed to. Being afraid is the thing that filled bellies and kept hearts beating. To live without fear was to not live at all. That night was no different to any other, and when the light from the sky burned down in the deep black night it was fear that boiled their blood and sent them fleeing from their bed. But the light was coming from all sides and the heat was searing the bushes and scorching the dry earth. Then came the voice. They could not say whether the voice had form, for it did not come from a mouth or throat (for it had none), and seemed to echo all around the mountain, inside their ears, sending ripples through their bones. "Be not afraid."

As their eyes adjusted in the blazing white light, they saw it almost fully: an object suspended in air, burning like a flame. It was aloft between six limbs edged with white filament, and its many eyes spun like stars. No legs or hands or face or anything remotely human, it glided against the wind towards and above them. The crackling of the branches catching fire grew to a roaring blaze. All the heat and noise and unbearable light; they cried out in a fear they had never known before. "Be not afraid," they heard over the inferno. The blaze was as high as the visitor now and the mountain shone red like wine and blood. The smoke blackened and swirled but could not conceal the visitor in all its great luminosity. Its voice was like song. "Be not afraid." At last they stood at full height and stared down the floating eyes, the whiteness, the heat of it all, and all at once the flames extinguished; the bushes had burned black and skeletal under the newly-black sky. Their eyes met and they found their words: "Here I am."

WATER FROM THE WELL

Dry. Dry.

The second time this week the water ran putrid and dark; the smell sour and revolting. They went to turn the tap back but found resistance: the grime crunched in the threads and they forced it closed with a grunt. Sighing, they turned behind them and called: "I'm going to the well. There's something wrong again."

"Maybe something died down there," a voice called back.

"Certainly smells like it" they muttered under their breath.

"What was that?"

"Nothing. I'm going now."

By some good fortune, the rains had stopped, if only for a moment, and the clouds parted to make way for thin strips of sunshine over the rocky hills. They took their chances and left their coat inside. Outside the air was fresh and pleasant, sweet from rain. The well itself was not far from the house but a recent rainfall made for unsteady ground and their boots were worn smooth from so many journeys. Gently, they made their way down the scree of the hill towards the little makeshift shelter – a mere slate roof standing on two rough planks – plenty enough for the well to be spared the salt and grit the winds carry, or the unfortunate gifts from birds flying overhead. They were surprised to find no one else standing over it to investigate: the last time, they and the neighbours stood, hands on hips, glaring into the dark pit of the well as if some spectral explanation were to appear before them if only they willed it so. Perhaps the neighbours had not drawn water today. Perhaps they had and their water was fine. Perhaps their house had an unfortunate break in the pipe. Perhaps it was just them this time.

They made their way over to the edge of the well and peered over the brink, squinting hard into the gloom. They could see no movement: in fact, the blackness was perfectly still. But black it was. Like staring into the night when the stars are clouded over, like liquid charcoal oozing from a fire that has been burning too long. The smell made them grimace and, pulling the length of their skirt over their face, leaned hard over the edge and into that strange precipice. *Something must have died,* they thought, *and it's stinking out the whole damned water.* Slipping back over the edge and back onto hard ground, they glanced about for signs of approaching neighbours, but none came. As thin sheets of rain returned, they pondered their situation. They had enough water to last them the next two days if used modestly enough, and perhaps further down the hill the neighbours had even more to spare. They were the closest to town – surely others had reported a corpse festering in the well – and so they decided to clamber up the hill again, now quickly running slick with wet clay, and return home. *With luck,* they thought, *enough rain will flush out the problem.*

When they came to the door their companion was already waiting for an explanation.

"What's wrong with the well?"

"I'm sopping. Let me dry off first," they growled, settling down by the fire they had let fade to cold. They tossed some fistfuls of dry paper into the embers.

"Well?"

"Well. I couldn't see. But there's definitely something there. It stinks like death." The boots were drenched in rain and muck; they took more paper from beside the fire and stuffed them inside.

"What do we do?"

"Have a little faith." They reached out a cold hand and touched their companion's face. "All will be well."

Rotten. Rotten.

A third time, a fourth, a fifth, and now rotten, putrid sludge spluttered from the faucet. The rust and grime congealed into a foul residue that made them choke. They recoiled from the sink in disgust, pressing a hand into their nose. "It's all wrong," they said, "Why haven't they done anything? How is it worse?"

They gathered themself and ground the tap to a groaning stop. "It must be the residue left before the water runs clear. Let me check the... the pipes". Pulling on their hardened boots they left the door open behind them so as to let the fresh air clear the house. *It must be us. It can't be the water. It must be the* – But the pump was sitting atop its perch like always and the pipes were not cracked or rusted or ruined. They drew a long, slow breath to still themself. Then they took off down the hill.

The earth was red with clay now and all boot prints had been swept away in the rainfall. From the peak of the hill they could see the well swelling with water, black like ink and just as bitter, bubbling over the rim as if alive with eels. Over the wind they could hear the thing babbling like a hellmouth, belching and breathing as the curdling waters carried on down the slope. The rocks were tarred in strings of it all like a bleeding mass running dark blood through knuckles and gristly cartilage. The smell, the smell. The air of rotting things, lungfulls of it, sighing out of the mouth of the well. They felt their scalp wet with sweat and oil. They pulled their whole skirt up to their face and couldn't care that they were exposed up there on the peak and the hot, stagnant air brushed their skin like an unwanted hand.

For a moment they did nothing. Then, catching themselves, bundled their skirt down to their knees and sped down the hill towards the neighbours' house. It was just down the way, and surely, they could smell the foul air from where the house stood, and surely they knew already, and surely help was on the way. Surely, they would arrive to find the men, tools in hand and masks up to their eyes, trudging up the slope to meet them. Surely. Please.

Upon approach, they saw strange plumes curling up from their roof, and all at once their desperate hope turned to desperate terror. The black up the walls, the black in the thatching, the earth outside. They stood on the edge of inaction before pelting towards the charred remains of the building. When the wall of foulness hit their face, they stopped dead again, dared not go any further, and retreated back the way they came.

Their thoughts raced: *is home next? Ought I to run straight home or to the town to fetch help? But the town is so far, and I should first tell them where I intend to go, or else...* They felt their feet halt in the mud, then turn abruptly towards the river.

The river was a mere mile and a half from home, a hard walk trudging through rain-soaked mud and even harder in the winter ice, but they ran as hard as they could, pushing arms through trees, catching skin on brambles, swallowing gulps of air still stained with the flavour of the well. In time thin streams trickled by their feet and they knelt to cup handfuls of the water to their mouth: they were so glad to taste its freshness they laughed aloud. They paused to wash their face off, poured some into their hair and wrung it out over the forest floor. They were still wiping the water from their eyes when they arrived at the clearing where the river ran closest. It was there that they stopped, and they did not move again.

They were looking into the eyes of it as it crouched in the waters; its eyes already fixed on them. They looked into it and it looked back at them. For a long time neither of them made a sound; the river babbled softly as they stared into one another.

Eventually its mouth opened, black and gory, thick with mottled blood and tar that trickled down as its edges turned upwards into a smile. It held its mouth this way while it convulsed, vibrating in the water, hind legs obscured by the disturbed silt. It let out a sound – long and low, deranged. They could not make a sound, but tears started in their eyes and they felt fear run in liquid down their legs. The tone endured. They finally conjured the courage to sob. Their cries were barely a whisper, but it ceased its noise at once to listen, smiling again. Its maw moved about as if to attempt challenging new sounds. Its lips pursed and the tar cracked where it had dried. "H. H. Hu – *Human.*"

They gasped. It tilted its head to the side, vibrating still, but now it was crouching further into the water, further into the murky clouds forming at its feet. They trembled at the thought of how large it must be at full height as even crouched low like a dog it was taller than them on the bank. "Humannn," it continued (it seemed to enjoy seeing them cry) "don't you know me?"

"Yes, I do" they whispered, and braced themselves as it started to extend its arms through the water in a wide arc.

"Then you know what you must do."

"I don't. I don't know what you want."

It let out a cackle that sounded like cracked glass as it rose out of the water and onto its hooves. The size of it struck them cold and sweaty but they were mesmerised awake to bear it. As it came towards them, they saw its form and trembled. It was not to be seen. Unholy thing, a forbidden thing. They were desperate to flee but was captivated by it, as if it willed them to stand and witness it rising from its watery pit, to see it fully, unbridled, as they should never have done. To see what should be unseen. Their prayers raced in their mind. They called upon all things in the forest to come to their aid but all they heard was its voice: "Then I will show you."

It reached out a hand and pulled them by the hair deep into the water, something of theirs cracking on the rocks below, and they could do nothing but watch the red curl like smoke in the current. It was hard to tell in the rush and the river which parts of them felt pain and which were still intact. They could not struggle; it was as it willed. They watched their breath escape in rhythmic bubbles up to the surface and break like rain. When they finally fell limp it cradled them in its hands, too large, too hot, out from the riverbed where they could see now their hair was slick and heavy with black water, and the same sludge was in their mouth, between their teeth, in their eyelashes, sticking and stinking. It traipsed through the trees in too-wide strides – it had claimed the land as its domain now – and out into the exposed hillside where the well stood seething in its own rancid heat. It looked into their eyes and smiled again. There was just enough left in them to look back into it and plead without words. A long, hooked tongue, barbed like a cat, slithered from its mouth over them. It savoured them for a moment, then lifted them high over the well. All at once they were in the blackness and heat, writhing over them, consuming them. Their eyes were clogged with it; they tried to breathe but lungfulls poured into them. They drank it until they were full, swallowing down the putrid mass, until there was no more they could contain. They swallowed it down and down until they were swollen with water, til the light closed around them and they sank deeper away from it as it watched from the rim. When it was satisfied, it saw a house further up the hill where a person was watching, aghast. "What's in the well?" they asked at length.

It smiled sweetly; the form of a human headed back towards the house. Their voice trilled over the wind: "You can come down. The water is good."

LEVIATHAN

The Bosun was already out of sight as they fell, limbs whirling, into the maw. The crew fell like rain around them and their cries harmonised into a ringing choir of terror and fear. The sea was a perch for the limbs that came down with noise like thunder upon the deck, and the ship cracked in two. Those that remained aboard the wreckage leapt to their chances in the icy water or else drew their pistols. In the fall that felt like eternity, they could see bursts of gunpowder clouds erupting on the fast-sinking wreck – some towards the beast, some to their own temples: they collapsed like ragdolls, sliding down the deck and into the ocean after their struggling, swimming shipmates. All the world was ending in a torrent of salt and blood.

The maw was open like a hellmouth, rotating in red and with the stench of rotting things, and they landed, colliding with one another into the heat and the dark. Then everything went black.

When the mate came to, the Bosun was weeping loudly in the corner, propped up against another body. Someone else – it was so hard to see in the gloom – was striking damp matches on a matchbox. Flimsy sparks spluttered from their hands and faded quickly, giving brief flashes of light in the deep, hot darkness. The absurdity of this foreign landscape could not yet strike fear into the mate – there was simply too much to take in – and small sparks of thought rose and fell in their mind like so many damp matches. When they tried to move, pain rippled across their shoulders and they winced loudly.

"You're still alive?"

"Seems like it," the mate said. Their mouth was dry with seawater. "Where are we?"

"The mouth," replied the Bosun between sobs, "Or maybe the belly."

"It can't be the belly, or we'd already be dead," the match-striker said.

"We're already dead."

"I didn't think Purgatory so hot, or Hell so empty. Are you certain there's no matchbox in your pocket? These are soaking; there's no use." As if the box itself was listening, they struck a dry match with a rip through the grain and a small globe of light grew from the tip of the match like a miracle. They held it aloft like a godly thing. In the modest glow of the matchlight they could see the edges of their shipmates lined in orange: some of them still with mouths and eyes open with their terrible final expressions still etched on their faces. They smelled of hot meat. In silence they cast their eyes over them in sorrow, then the match-striker's eyes fell upon the hip of one of their comrades. They leapt up and the match extinguished itself in the rush. The second darkness seemed so much deeper than the first. As if the temptation of meagre light had made them all greedy to see.

In the new dark there was a moment of fast movement and prayer then, with a squeak and clatter of metal, the chasm opened up in warm light. The match-striker stood with the lit oil lamp, triumphant, which quickly gave way to loss and terror. The lamp cast a warm glow over the corners of where they had fallen: a peristaltic form of flesh, cave-like and cavernous in its volume but alive with movement, stinking and sighing and monstrous. In new light they saw those piles of torn bodies piled up along the edges, some half-tumbled down, some still mangled in the rows of teeth further along the wall. They were sure they had seen so many perish in the wreck or leap to their deaths in the sea, but here the number of bodies before them seemed infinite. So many rotted and scorched, blistered and mauled. It took so long for them to realise because the truth was so terrible: there were too many bodies here to be just from their ship – these bodies were older, swallowed long ago. This creature was old. So old, ancient and ruthless. An impossible thing. It had not even cared to swallow them completely: these were human lives left half-chewed, stuck in a jaw so large it could go on consuming and never be satiated. They were krill on the tongue of a whale.

Silence and solemnness swallowed them. Then the Bosun began sobbing harder. It was a wailing, mewling noise that drove yet more despair into the cavern. They were a honeycomb of open mouths, the dead and the weeping. The match-striker, now nursing the lamp-light, began treading in circles over the spongy floor beneath them and stopped at a tunnel-like appendage that followed deep down inside the abdomen of the body, and hideous bursts of hot air forced them to recoil. The immediacy of death hung over them. They thought of how their bodies would not be found, how they would never see the sky again. The world rotated around them in glorious splendour above the foaming sea while they sat quietly to await their doom. They wondered if they were below the waves again, or perhaps it had crawled over the rocks and was slithering to land to eat and eat without end. How long until that maw reopened, and more souls poured in?

Propped up on corpses, they could see the Bosun's legs were shattered, too mangled to splint. How were they crying for so long? The lamp-holder began pacing circles again, working through their denial aloud: "This is the mouth; that tunnel must be the throat. If it swallows again, we'll be forced down into God-knows-what. Or maybe when its mouth opens again, we could make a break for it."

"I'm doomed," wailed the Bosun, "You can't carry me. Just throw me into the belly."

"Nonsense," snapped the light-bearer, "We're getting out. We are all getting out."

They both looked at the mate, who until now had remained perfectly silent. "You awake?"

"I don't know," they said.

"What do you have?"

The question seemed foolish. Politely, so as not to upset their station, the mate patted over their body and placed each item they found in front of them like humble offerings at a feast. "A dagger. My penknife. My flask. Matches…Wet matches." The mate sat beside the Bosun and gently lifted the flask to their lips. The Bosun took a trickle of it and smiled. "I was expecting water." It was the first time they had stopped crying. Then they erupted into laughter. When they stopped, they pressed the neck of the flask back up to their lips. The Bosun looked wearily into their face. "That's very good."

"It's spiced," the mate said quietly, "I drink it when I need courage."

"Perhaps you should drink some now."

"I don't think courage is what I need right now," they replied. "W-with respect."

The lamp-holder scoffed. "then what? What is it? You're making *peace* now?" They rattled the lamp like a threat. "You see how much oil we have left? *Minutes.* And we are getting out of – I'll be damned – I'll be *damned* – if I die here. So, you listen here, *mate*, we are taking what we have and we are getting out of here."

"I'm sorry, but this is it. We are not getting out of this alive."

"Then you should have just jumped overboard if you were gonna be so damned cowardly!" The lamp-holder produced a pistol (and a dribble of seawater) from their hip and held it out at arms length. Standing there with lamp and pistol aloft they appeared like a seafaring Michael, light and lance and flaming blade, to wreak terrible vengeance upon them. But in the deep red bowels of the monster, the pistol was transformed: it was no more threatening to them than a lily held out to their face. The mate's lack of fear irritated the lamp-holder; they stormed closer and the muzzle was pressed to the mate's forehead now, refreshingly cool in the hot, breathy air.

"Don't you dare. Stand down" the Bosun barked, and the lamp-holder's eyes flamed with rage.

"You don't deserve to try to carry on out of here if you're just giving up like that. If you want to die, let me help you. We'll just be on our way out when that mouth opens again. You'll see."

"You'll do no such thing!" the Bosun cried.

They pressed their forehead harder into the cold kiss of the pistol and looked into the lamp-holder's eyes. They thought for a moment before saying, quite calmly, "I am making my peace in this terrible place. If you take my whiskey, my tools, my life, I shall not begrudge you. If you are sure you can escape, please try. But please do not make the Bosun suffer simply because you are afraid to die."

The lamp-holder inhaled slowly and struck them hard across the face with the butt of the pistol. The mate slumped against the floor and the Bosun screamed with rage and agony, paralysed against the bodies of their comrades. "How dare you!" The lamp-holder was half-screaming, and the light swirled around the cavern as they recoiled from the blow. "We survived for a *reason*! We have been given another chance to live! You think *they* didn't deserve a chance to live?!" They ran the light over the lifeless faces around them; the Bosun wailed again. "You think they didn't deserve a chance? You think they wouldn't try to escape if they could? But yet here *you* are – "They paused to kick the mate in the side, "–quitting before you've started. *Pathetic.*"

The mate did not attempt to rise from the floor. "The universe is indifferent," they said quietly, "There is nothing but chaos; there is no such thing as 'deserve'. They died, we lived, and now we will die too."

The lamp-holder spat. There was a bitter silence that hung in the air, thicker than the blood coagulated in pools around them. The lamp-holder watched the flame drink the oil down. For a moment the three of them sighed the hot air, then the two of them knew at once the Bosun was gone. Saying nothing, they moved in agreement – the unspoken law among all people – and gently pushed the Bosun's eyelids closed. They had died weeping. Solemnity washed over them like a still sea; the Bosun's shroud covered them all alike. The lamp-holder set the light down and turned it to show the last trickles of oil. "Peace," they said.

"Peace."

The lamp-holder reached out to the mate and wiped the blood from their lips; they did not flinch. All past conflict was over with. Tears did not start in their eyes for there was no need. The knife and pistol stayed untouched on the floor behind them, no more relevant to them now than the food on their tables back home. Meals forever uneaten, books unfinished, words not spoken. Everything seemed washed away in sea water. In the dimming light, the mate offered up the flask to the lamp-holder, which they took in silent thanks. In the midst of violent peristalsis, they were two solemn cornerstones, lighthouse keepers in the tempest. The whiskey was sweeter than anything before it, washing away blood, salt and bile. When the elixir was exhausted, they held each other, each looking into the other: they were one another's anchors at sea. They traced each other's features as the light flickered, flickered, and finally faltered. All was dark. The darkness was deeper than ocean, and twice as black. It could have been a bed in summer, a moonless night.

There was a noise like bellowing wind, and then the maw opened: the cold washed in, and all was swept into endless sea.

SOLVE COAGULA

This isn't what I wanted when I said I wanted something new.

They were charming enough, sure. Alert eyes, indifferent tone. They bought me a drink and I let them. It had been an age since the breakup and I was determined to prove something, I suppose – I just wasn't sure what that was exactly. For the first few weeks I just drank, celebrated my small freedoms (I went where I liked – my choice was always the first choice – and I didn't have to tell anyone where I was or what I was up to) and confused my near constant drinking for freedom: I assumed this was just what free people did. That particular night I'd decided to slow my pace, maybe take up a hobby, but was determined to pick someone up as a final conquest. I'd never had a one-night stand before and hadn't a clue how to approach it. I wore something black and assumed that was enough to indicate my intentions. I went alone and spoke to no one, sunken into my chair. As the night wore on, I became less and less hopeful. My loneliness hung over me like a dark cloud.

Walking home alone when you expect someone on your arm is a different kind of quiet. My arm was still crooked as if I was expecting someone to take it. The streets were empty and nauseatingly quiet. I craved life. As if answering my prayer, I heard the thumping of music drift over on the breeze, and I followed the sound like a bloodhound. I arrived at a packed bar, bright with glass, and someone by the door stopped me before I had stepped a foot over the threshold. "Can I buy you a drink?" I couldn't play coy if I tried. I turned, grinning, to find them smoking behind me (I hate smoking). They stomped it out beneath their shoe and spirited me inside.

Conversation was dry. In fact, no amount of liquid courage could make it flow. They were an accountant, or a lawyer, or something, but I couldn't remember. As inebriated as I was even, I was uncomfortable. I couldn't believe it had come to this. "Do you come here often?"

"Huh?"

I was shouting but I wasn't sure if I needed to. I had no grasp of how busy it was in there. "Do you come here a lot? To this place?"

"Oh. I'm not sure if I'd say 'a lot'."

"Have you come here before though?"

"Yes."

"Well, I haven't. I've never seen this place before."

There. That conversation was dead too. We had truly scraped the bottom of the barrel. I had no idea what they wanted. A brick wall would be a better talking companion. Then they looked at me with eyes like fire and said, "You want to get out of here?" I let them take my hand and lead me out into the street.

They pushed me awake. Their arms were hard. Half-sleeping and still misty from drink I pushed back playfully, but then they gripped me hard and I snapped to attention. They were standing over me, only now their human form was shed like snakeskin in the bed; its limp, empty fingers like gloves still draped over me. I screamed and they stopped me with a fist in my mouth. The taste of earth and ash crackled on my tongue. I wasn't trying to scream now. I was *furious*, swearing and biting against their hand and flailing my own fists about in a feeble effort to hurt them back. Their put a second hand over my mouth, then a third, then a *fourth*. My muted screams were shredding my throat. They started shushing – I think it was shushing – me but the sound that escaped their mouth was low and guttural, staccato rumble. I fell silent.

"Stop struggling," they said in a voice that was so different to their human counterpart, "You will do as I say now."

I nodded, quietly. They released all four arms, peeled back like fruit skin, and sat down upon me. Their hair, course and hot, brushed my skin and I suddenly became acutely aware of how small and soft I seemed below them. I tried not to stare too long at their parts, their face, beastly and bearded, their many unfolding hands. They looked long and hard at me before speaking again.

"You will obey, now. Or you shall die. You shall choose now."

I was stuttering. I'd never stuttered before. The words fell before me like shattered glass and I couldn't piece them together in my mouth. Finally, I managed to force out, in ashy breath: "Obey."

I married them in blood and fire. They baptized me in the river. When they pulled me up from the water everything felt colder. I could not eat. I took up smoking. I watched them pull human skin over themselves every morning and leave the house. In the day I paced the floors, restless, and scoured the house for a key to release myself (I found nothing). The neighbours would walk by every day and waved sweetly as I beat the glass with my open hands, sobbing. I wondered if they saw me – but then again, why would they wave if they could not see me through the window? I'd taken fire pokers to that glass, swung chairs over my head at it, all in vain. When I finally gave in to the windows, I tried the doors, took up lock-picking, took up carpentry, took up axe-wielding. I tried every day for hours on end until there was nothing left to try. I lay on the kitchen floor, wailing aloud to myself, glaring at the ceiling. It was grazed from horns.

When they returned home in the evenings, they would sometimes stay human for a while, eat bloody steak and play with matches. Other times they were barely through the door before they shrugged off their skin and kicked it across the floor in a sopping heap. In their true form, they mostly sat. They barely moved. Tranquil as a monk, they would sit for hours on end simply breathing. I watched them, waiting to catch them out but they stayed with eyes fixed to the wall, unblinking. Sometimes I would sit directly in front of them, cross my legs and stare as hard as I could back, inviting them to falter or else transport me with them to wherever they had drifted off to.

We spoke little. Conversation was dry as ash, and I wondered every day on the "obey". We had barely exchanged words since my arrival. They stayed in their private rotation and I in mine. They lived their life outside the walls. I simply existed in the house like their chosen ghost. I haunted my polycerate host for months without end.

One day they did not come home. I waited solemnly by the door like a dog. I chain-smoked a pack of cigarettes, then another; I stubbed the dead ends out on the carpet in defiance. I hated them for leaving me here. Alone.

The door swung open in the early hours and four feet stepped over my sleeping body. I awoke to see that this time they were with company: a human being, I was sure of it. They were haunted looking, not yet as thin as I was, and the fragrance of spiced liquor wafted over them. They pointed them to the bathroom. A bizarrely normal exchange. We heard the rush of the tap through the door, and when it stopped there was a pause before they returned to us. My companion peeled back their skin and whispered to me "Remember what you promised".

The bedroom was melancholy, thick with hatred. I stared at the newcomer, saying nothing, wondering how they were not more disturbed by the horned, winged creature before them. They were looking back at me, and my companion was looking greedily back at *them*. We stood in a triangle of eyes. For a long time, no one moved, then finally the newcomer stepped forward to leave and was thrown across the room in a flurry of feathers and goat hair, slamming hard against the headboard, head rocking in shock. There were hands on hands on hands, hooves on the bedsheets; I backed against the wall and watched in horror. The newcomer kept their eyes on me all the while, silently begging, and I was disgusted with myself. The beast looked at me too, jaw gaped and grunting hot breath, as if to say *you are complicit.*

The house was growing busy in the ensuing months. I became thin as a tooth; I wished to disappear into air. They made a habit of collecting people – where from, it was impossible to tell – and so the house gradually filled with footfall and thinning human bodies. Each time a person was plucked out from the world and brought here we watched silently, did not avert our eyes, would not raise a hand to stop them. Maybe we were all to blame, after all. I watched the newcomers struggle to escape, scream at the waving passers-by for help, and I let them. They needed to learn for themselves the futility of hope. They shook me but I bent like a reed. In time, their desperate hope faded to bitter acceptance: they joined me in silence. We ate from the floor. We bathed together like snakes. We shed our humanity like they shed theirs at the door. We were ghosts together. We breathed and sighed in the walls. We did not speak of the before-time.

In time, we became legion. They became greedy: our numbers rose in exponential bounds. Soon there were too many bodies for chairs, so we took turns sleeping on the floor. When our ranks increased, there was no room to lie down so we took to standing. We stood cheek to cheek, became stone, would not move. In time there were so many of us they had to barge through us to get to the door. Soon enough there was no room for them to extend their limbs and be rid of their human skin. They stayed in their body and became sickly and pale. They left the house every morning and returned in a sweat, as if they could not be contained in that soft little shell.

The final night, they left with their coat and we knew that two people would be returning through the door later that night. In their hubris, they did not foresee our fraternity: our separation, our coming together. We turned like shifting scales towards the door and waited. We were pale as water, thin as rain. But in our multitudes, we became ocean. We bore like the tide. When the door finally clicked open, we were still awake: a hundred eyes were upon them. they had to force the door open to get through, hooked a shoe round its edge to keep it wedged open, and then their eyes met ours. We were a thousand lights on fire in a shifting sea. Their newest companion saw the seething insides of the house, shrieked, and fled; in their feeble human form they were powerless to stop them. We saw fear pass over them for the first time.

I watched one of us pass through the door, easy as silk. They were astonished into silence. Then, they all followed: flowing like water through the crack in the door, pushing them to the ground, washing over them, making no sound. Our bare feet touched the cool night and we breathed through our skin.

I was the last one left behind. Without the hoards teeming inside the walls, the house seemed so empty now, and a kind of quiet that seemed so pitiful and sad. The wallpaper was cast blue in the moonlight, and I felt swallowed in the glow. I had all the space in the world, it seemed, and for a long time I simply stood in the centre of it all, just being. A profound nothingness. I considered this two-bed terrace my kingdom: us and us alone, tangled together in hatred. I unravelled our fate before me on the floor and saw the map trail off into clotting capillaries of time.

My strange companion watched me from where they lay. An unspoken dialect burned through the barbed thread that connected the two of us and all at once the spell was broken. I looked at the door, split open like an eye, and I walked through it. The street was silver with moonlight and serenaded by late birds chattering and whistling in the dark. I looked over my shoulder as they began picking at their fingertips, pulling their human glove from their claws. I put my naked foot down on their hand, looked them dead in those rectangle eyes and said "Obey."

6

Mornings on the coast were curtained in mist. Every morning dense fog rolled in from the sea and cast a shroud of otherworldly melancholy over all things: the shadows were mottled and misty, the trees and earth seemed grey, like all the world was charcoal.

This morning was no different. They woke to unseasonal chill – but after all, what was seasonal anymore? – and lit the stove for hot water. Cold mornings made them crawl out of sleep in a daze; everything seemed to move slower and sleepier. As the kettle purred on the stove they hauled on their coat and boots, heavy like oppressive mist, and drew the curtains wide. The sky threatened rain. Behind them, the whistle of the kettle snapped them to attention. Hot coffee went down like an elixir in the cold, and they brought the mug out with them into the cold morning. The stones crunched underfoot in the shadow of the cliff face: the footfalls through the stony beach were the heartbeat of the forager. Under the watchful eye of the cliff, the kiss between shore and land, they felt a part of something colossal and ancient. They were so small in the face of such gargantuan history it was as though they were not truly present at all: a mere witness in a brief moment of sentience in an ocean of unfathomable time. The sea was angry: it seethed and spoke in baritone over the wind. The earth, layered in deep stripes along the cliff, stood sentry to the sky and sea. Ancient, lovely thing. Grain like skin. Fractures like laughter lines. They blessed the adhesed rock like Gaia and carried on down the beach, drinking as they went. They spied a piece of driftwood and claimed it as a walking stick; they admired its twisted form as they strode on.

Sometimes, happening upon something wrong is too subtle to tell. Sometimes, the mind wishes the happening away, buries it deep, refuses it. This time, though, they knew at once something was wrong. They knew this land, this corroded cliff, this unforgiving sea. They had walked this shoreline without end and never come across such a thing.

The crack – a fissure in the soft tissue in the body of the cliff – was wide as a wave and just as severe. They looked into it like a tear in time. It looked as though two great hands had ripped the fabric of the rock in twain; the fresh split in the earth bled ashy breath. A dreadful splinter in the cosmos.

Peering in, they saw nothing foreign in the cavity, just a smell like chalk. They wondered about what strange fossils they might find if it were prized further open, and for a moment the greed of the thought made their mouth water. But the quiet respect of the land centred them, and they walked slowly off, still watching the fracture over their shoulder for fear any moment it would move, split open wider, and some terrible creatures would slither out. They watched it until it shrank out of sight.

When they returned along the beach late that afternoon, shouldering a haul of bounty plucked from the rocks, the schism welcomed them back like a half-open eye. It seemed to follow them all along the shoreline, all the way home. When the house was finally in sight they broke into a run, stones skipping under their boots, clumsily fumbled their keys out of their pocket and slammed the door behind them. They prepared bread and tea and watched suspiciously through the window out to the cliff: they didn't trust it not to move. They swore it was listening, for it refused to shift. When they finally sunk their tea and finished the bread, they were still unsatisfied. They dared for something to appear in the rock, they willed it so. But the cliff gave no surrender and stood, tall and grim, and the split in the rock remained.

The evening time was madness. The sea picked up into a foaming flurry in the hard winds and the early fog hardened into thick cover of cloud. In the pale light the discontinuity was murky and obscure. Often in the time before the schism you could catch a glimpse of boat lights blinking on the dark horizons, or, closer, the clicking of bats zipping overhead. This night was eerily still and heavy with the threat of rain still not come: the worst conditions for spying precious delights amongst the rocks and pools on the beachfront. Today's harvest was meagre; they blamed the fracture for their poor fate. As the sheets of rain came, they put another pot of tea on to steep and decided tonight was a lost cause. They pressed the cup to their lips and swore they spied movement out in the storm.

The night was lush with soothing noise: shushing rain and hushing sea rolling in and out on the singing pebbles. They lay in their bed listening like a child in the womb. They tried to forget the lacerated rock. They tried not to imagine horrible visions crawling out of it and into the swirling sea. They drank in the ocean sighs and songs like medicine on their muscles pulled tense in uncertainty.

The sun shone blistering and oppressive over their face and they raised a hand over their eyes to shield from the glare. Had they fallen asleep in the storm? Had they woken to the high midday sun? They dropped their hand and touched something cold and scaly. They started. Scurrying back from whoever was lying beside them, they beheld the form of a mercreature all toothy and barbed. Its eyes were marbled and depthless, pluckable, and its lips curled back from its white gums. They looked down upon themselves for fear its tail still slithered over them, intertwined in their legs, but no relief came from seeing the pair were separate. Their belly was bulged, and they felt something – something alive – flittering inside them. Pain moved down them in a wave and a thousand slithering, chittering things crawled out from between their legs. Screaming triumphantly, the creatures slid out onto the pebbled beach and made for the sea in a sliming, mewling exodus.

They awoke with a start. It was still night. The sunlight was just the moon beaming in through a crack in the curtains; they were awash in its cool light.

They half-dozed 'til morning, too wary to sleep for fear of falling back into the old dream. They neglected the stove and left the house hungry. They stormed back over to the cracked rockface and glared into it to make certain it had not changed. Brave with hatred, they scored the cracked earth with their hands. They could feel no alien presence, no paranormal signature in the shattered grain. So how had this come to be? They stared down the stretch of the beach and the image of yesterday's stone harvest bloomed in their mind.

Crunch. They stabbed the beam into the pebble stones and deep into the sand beneath. *Crunch.* They know this beach better than their own body. *Crunch.* They would not allow this uninvited smile upon the rock. *Crunch.* Satisfied with the makeshift tent they had erected, they then set about digging a pit for a fire, a spit, a humble bed. They neglected their beloved beach and set themself down as stone watchman before the schism, shoulders hunched and eyes unforgiving. They took no supper and put upon themselves this new dedication: the knight before the cliff.

The wind was cruel and sharp, but they held steadfast in the shelter. They shook in the cold and gritted their teeth. They would not be swayed from the watch. They made a silent oath – they swore on the sea – to stand guardian of this rock and their beloved beach from any foul disturbance that might befall it. When the tide rolled in it battered them against the cliff and they clung to the rock as sanctuary, their fingers locked tight in the fracture, and endured the water for hours without end. They watched crumbs of rock come away from the cliff and be eaten by the sea. They wondered when something would rise from the depths and devour them too. In the battering that was unrelenting, their dreams became realised as the sea ate greedily into the discontinuity. It cleaved open like a mighty earthen wound, and another wave forced them inside the raw rock. They cried out, defiant against the rage of the sea, and held and held and held.

In the ensuing tide, they became sea-like: their hair was locked with seagrass and weeds, eyes red from salt, body cut from lacerating sand and shell. They felt carved by the waters as much as the cliff itself but felt awash with shame for not being able to defend the fault-line. It was wide like an open mouth now, and deep enough for them to have holed up inside it to defend from the storm. They forgot their watch for merfolk. They were exhausted, cold, empty with hunger. But still they could not bring themselves to return to the house. The visions of the slithering brood returned to them and their resolve burned once more. *Only the sea,* they thought, *only the sea can move me.*

Their clothes became seafoam; their fingernails were barnacled and cockle shelled. They accepted the fate of the half-creature, for the sea had baptised them in thanks. They clung on to the rock and swore to themselves they would not become driftwood. Any more than they would be the oceanic surrogate *thing.*

On the third day, the weather subsided. The wind fell to a breath on their cheek and the splashing cacophony of the tide receded into whispering song. The salt stung their cuts as it cleaned them: the sea's furious kisses. The very rock they were protecting had been hurled back in a flurry at them. *I am testing you,* whispered the sea out in its low tide, *for you are an honourable guard.* They were sprawled in a heap over the exposed rock, finally laying their head back. They allowed themselves rest. When they saw movement in their closing eyes, they refused it: it was simply a figment of a storm-battered imagination, a tired mind. Let it be.

But the movement continued past the point of excusion and they found themselves face-to-face with a masked thing, pale and slender and they *thought* human, pulling itself from the depths of the cliff. Its body was encased in rock and it doused itself in the meagre pools by their feet but could not be free. It turned to the sea and – "*No!*" cried the watchman, but the cliff creature was already away towards the shore. They tried to give chase, but it was already loose: it slipped its rocky binds to expose its body, quite perfect, serene in the calm, and began walking back towards the cliff. "No," they said again, and they couldn't tell whether letting them go or having them come closer was the lesser of two evils. Tenderly it moved towards the watchman, took their torn hands (they winced) and brought them over their neck, their breasts, their belly, their face. The watchman stood aghast and did not resist. They said, "Take off that mask."

"There is no mask," it replied.

"What are you?"

It did not reply. Silently, it studied the watchman's body with its fingers – quite delicately, with admiration – considered their state from enduring the harsh gifts of the unforgiving sea. It explored their face with both hands. It fingered their wounds, they exposed red flesh (they thought it might like them like an animal, but they could see no mouth) and studied the blood on its fingertips. Finally satisfied, it stepped forward again and pressed its body against them in a long embrace. They breathed in the chalk of its sin, smooth like marble. When the alabaster creature finally pulled away from them its mask was shed: instead a familiar human face, quite healed and glowing with health, remained. They gasped and tried to cry out for help, but their mouth was covered. Covered in layers of rock. Sand foamed and frothed on the tongue. They leapt after it in rage as if to snatch back their stolen face with their bare hands but found themselves utterly encased in stone – stripes of it, heavy and ancient and unending. The thief practiced a smile – and again, and again, and again, then said in a voice that did not belong to it: "How do I look?"

If rage were a light, they would have set the ocean ablaze. *That's my voice! You have my voice!* In vain they struggled against the rock forming faster and faster over them: a wall bricking itself up before their very eyes. A pit of salt and rock and festering blood, they screamed into the cliff as it closed around them. There was perfect silence on the cliff. The schism healed; the laceration gone; the storm passed. On the shoreline, away from the untouched rock, someone kicked the remains of a makeshift shelter down and made their way, trudging through the pebbles, to the little house along the beach. They stepped inside and locked the door behind them.

UN-ME

I stayed in the house. I slept on the floor. I grew smaller and smaller, nestling into the crevice between the bed and the wall, contorted to fit, refused food, ate air, tread so lightly I left no footprints. I averted my eyes and levitated like a dream. I was symbolic, I was unreal. Soon, I decided I would be dead, and I wouldn't need to think of tomorrow, of the time after that, the time after that. I retched every morning, and my chest burned a hole in the middle of itself. I wondered if I was leaving pools of my insides where I slept but somehow nothing leaked through that hole in my chest, no matter how large it grew. It felt like a fist flexing inside my ribcage. I cried quietly at night and laid awake to feel it all.

I heard songs where there were none. I felt oppressive air like so many hands pressing down on my skull. I stopped and wept open-mouthed at clouds of starlings swooping and undulating over me. I spied for messages from beyond. I asked questions out loud. I wrote letters. I became un-me.

Months passed in dreams and fantasies. I floated through time in a four-limbed vessel. I couldn't remember my journeys home. I vomited in public toilets. I put lit matches out on myself and rubbed alcohol into my wounds. Un-me. I couldn't feel my fingertips and I couldn't feel cutting. Everything was unconvincing, like a bad painting. I convinced myself I was not real. All the world became a ghost.

The Post-Humans came in streams like melting ice. They trod land on slender legs and ran, humming like a choir, through fields and streets of tarmac cracked with weeds. They claimed to be friends of the old folk, came with good tidings and tools of prosperity. The people retaliated with violence and abandon. We thought the Post-Humans were done with, gone like a wisp, and I couldn't care either way in this unreal world. What did I care if we were visited by the gods of yonder if all my life had already ended?

I wasn't looking for them when I found them. I had swallowed down a couple of sedative trays and walked my body into the woods. It was a cold night – I had chosen this one specifically – and I sat myself down in a stump shaped like a pelvis, shed my clothes, lay naked in its skeleton, unbirthed myself. I poured gin down my throat and waited.

If it wasn't for them, I wouldn't have known I'd fallen asleep so soon. I opened my eyes to see a beautiful thing of constant flux, a kaleidoscopic dance of form that waxed and waned against me. I thought they were nuzzling into me for warmth, but then a distinct sharpness stung my side, and I felt a warm ribbon run down my body, the warmth of my blood. I put a hand out to push it away but I was sluggish from the pills and the gin and the cold; I moved like a hibernating insect against them as they pushed harder into me. I cried out this time as they bit down into me. Acid rushed in my veins. My mind was shaking me awake but my body betrayed it. Desperate now, harder awake from the shock of pain, I manage to drop an elbow on it; it recoiled from the blow (I must have hit something, at least) and I had a moment to look down. My belly was torn, bright red in the dying light of day. The shadows stretched long and lazy in the sunset. I too was a shadow, stretching out slowly and listlessly, fading into obscurity. My eyes were heavy. My head was screaming at me now to sharpen, wake up, *wake up.* I grasped my side with one hand, propping myself up with the other. I could feel my wet meat under my fingers. My head swam and I forced down vomit. My foe was recovered and was beginning to circle like a cat, something like haunches up, something like teeth bared. I took a swing at it and lost my balance, dropping to the ferny floor with a yelp as it dove for me. It caught my crown in its jaw and a veil of blood fell in thin sheets over my eyes. *No. Not like this.* What was I doing? Why was I so desperate not to die now – like this? Why feel pride now, naked and cold? Why am I too proud to be eaten? Blinded in red, I swung a meagre fist upwards and hit something. *These organs are mine.* We, two floundering, dying creatures, faltering like flame, grappled under the lowering sun. The blood was in every corner of my eyes now and the salt and iron ran into my mouth; I spat and foamed like a mad thing as it reached into me and took another terrible bite. In the fire of pain, I felt my insides spill from behind shredded tendons. *I don't want this I don't want this I don't want this.* I could do no more. I slumped back against the stump, devoured in rhythmic rounds, head swaying, eyes rolling, I saw the sun crawl under the treeline and cl–

A terrible growling, a yelping, a roaring, howling torrent – impossible to say how many mouths – and a voice called a name frantically over and over. I couldn't place it, I couldn't... *Please.* There was a loud crackling of footfall through the undergrowth and the voice was crying for them to stop and then – like all at once the story lay ahead of them fully-formed and perfectly legible – they stopped crying and said with a rage like poison: "Good dog. Get it. *Get it.*"

There were hands, I remember hands, and my back had two coats passed over it. The colours swam and my eyes were hard with drying blood and dirt tossed up from the fray. I could smell my own body spilled out of its skin, and the panicked forcing of my mangled inside back inside my ribs like spilled meat.

When I came to, the car was rattling over potholes and my body was on fire with pain. I was draped and dripped over someone's backseat. "Thank God," they said, glancing over their shoulder from the wheel, "I wasn't sure you were going to wake up."

I said nothing. I saw that I was exposed, and shame washed over me. As if hearing these thoughts, they said "I won't ask you what you were doing out there like that. And frankly, it's not my business. All I know is, thank God we got there in time. I don't know how much longer you would have lasted with that – it doesn't bear thinking about. You're here. That's all that matters.

"I thought they'd all gone, done with. That one looked pretty measly, though. Must have thought all its birthdays had come at once when it saw you. You know, I never knew why they called them Post-Humans. They're not remotely human."

"They named themselves." I finally said, and I felt the heavy curtain of sleep pass over me. "It was dying. It was hungry, too." The evening melted. The engine was like a heartbeat and gentle sleep washed over me. My chest felt full.